# UNLOCKED

# UNLOCKED

Ryan G. Van Cleave

Walker & Company ✺ New York

*To Victoria, Valerie, and Veronica—with love and gratitude*

First published in the United States of America in March 2011
by Walker Publishing Company, Inc., a division of Bloomsbury Publishing, Inc.
www.bloomsburyteens.com

For information about permission to reproduce selections from this book, write to
Permissions, Walker BFYR, 175 Fifth Avenue, New York, New York 10010

Library of Congress Cataloging-in-Publication Data
Van Cleave, Ryan G.
Unlocked / Ryan G. Van Cleave.
p.     cm.
Summary: While trying to impress a beautiful, unattainable classmate, fourteen-year-old
Andy discovers that a fellow social outcast may be planning an act of school violence.
ISBN 978-0-8027-2186-0 (hc)
[1. Novels in verse. 2. School violence—Fiction. 3. Loneliness—Fiction.
4. High schools—Fiction. 5. Schools—Fiction.] I. Title.
PZ7.5.V36Un 2011        [Fic]—dc22        2010023296
ISBN 978-0-8027-2355-0 (pb)

Book design by Danielle Delaney
Printed in the U.S.A. by Quad/Graphics, Fairfield, Pennsylvania
2  4  6  8  10  9  7  5  3  1 (hc)
2  4  6  8  10  9  7  5  3  1 (pb)

All papers used by Bloomsbury Publishing, Inc., are natural, recyclable products
made from wood grown in well-managed forests. The manufacturing processes
conform to the environmental regulations of the country of origin.

# UNLOCKED

# THE BEGINNING

August arrived
with 90° heat
and high school
began at last,
meaning five hundred
were funneled
in from four
different junior highs,
meaning
no one really arrived
having anything
except a sweaty
eagerness
to belong,
meaning we all
felt equally
displaced.

A few dragged
old cliques along,
but like magnetism,
the rest found others.
The beautiful
found beautiful friends.
Jocks found jocks.
Nerds found nerds.
Band geeks found band geeks.

Drama queens found drama queens.
Cheerleaders found cheerleaders.

When it all settled into
the Monday/Friday grind,
that agonizing slowness
of a school year,
I found myself
                    alone,
          excluded,
along with three
others I couldn't
bring myself
to befriend—
Sue, Nicholas,
and Blake.

At least they
didn't have
their dad working
at the school
like I did.
That's who I
became:
     the janitor's son.

## SUE

Some days,
her hair was
lizard-belly green,
but more often,
it was pink like
it'd suffered a sunburn.
Sometimes navy blue,
sometimes violet.
Come November,
she'd shave it clean
to the white smoothness
of her skull.

She didn't hate me
any more
than she hated
everyone else.
She was equal
opportunity
angry.

# NICHOLAS

The fourth
in a family
of seven boys,
he just got
forgotten
regularly
and managed
to stay
that way.
    Like he could
    turn sideways
    and disappear.
        Like he had alien
        blood that turned
        him transparent.

Wasn't as if people
disliked him—
Nicholas simply got
overlooked.
No one asked him
to share their table
in the cafeteria.
No one asked him
to let them copy
his biology notes.

No one even *Bless you*'d
him when he sneezed,
like they didn't even
hear his enormous ACHOO!

How bad was it
to be simply ignored?
For a bookworm,
it probably wasn't
all that awful.

If only he liked
video games more
than reading at the library,
maybe we'd have
been friends.

# ME

I didn't make fun
of anyone.

People who
eat cheese sandwiches
     alone
on second base
of the softball field
during lunchtime
didn't crack jokes
to anyone
but themselves.

I hated my dad's
blue uniform,
his name
in mocking red
cursive:
*Hector.*

I had to wait
an hour for him
after everyone
else had flown home.

Sometimes I helped,
but mostly

I just pretended
to push a broom
and listened to my iPod
when he wasn't watching.

Some days,
he let me have
a Coke
from the machine
in the teachers' lounge—
they replaced the ones
in the lunchroom machine
with fruit drinks
and bottled water.

The kids called him
Mr. Clean.
They called me
Clean Junior,
or CJ
when they were
feeling
particularly
cruel
(often).

# HONESTY

I try to be
someone
who believes
in honesty,

but the truth
is that I can't
tell when
the world's really
out to flatten me,
or if it's just me
somehow
self-sabotaging
my own damn life.

Two years
of anger therapy
	(thanks for nothing,
	Dr. Zigler)
and that's all
I can say about
why my life's
a twisted knot
the size of a fist.

My name is Andy.

I'm fourteen.

I hate my life.

Some days I feel
so alone
that I might be
living inside
a shoe box
on the moon.

Some days
I don't feel
anything
at all.

# BLAKE

He was popular
   once,
the kids from
his middle school say.
Really popular.
TV-sitcom popular.

The kids from
my middle school
didn't care if it
was true or not.
But I was intrigued
by the idea of such
sudden, drastic change.
A metamorphosis.

They said he
could blast
a soccer ball
straight over
the south wing
of the school.

Could zing
a spitball faster
than you
could see.

Birthday parties
with trampolines,
BBQ pits, and
live rock bands;
he had friends.

Now Blake roamed
the yellow-tiled halls
of Jefferson High
by himself
and wore
a big green
army belt
looped twice
around his waist.

He didn't talk
to anyone,
not even
the teachers.
His old friends
avoided him.
The other outcasts
steered clear of him too.
Sue was too busy texting
to care.
Nicholas read comics

constantly,
never looking up
to see Blake
sitting solo.

Sometimes I
watched Blake
and I wondered
what he was thinking,
if he had dark dreams
like the ones
that shocked me
out of sleep,
but I didn't ask.

Still,
      even an outcast
      like me
      heard the rumors.

Everyone said . . .
everyone suspected . . .
everyone thought . . .
that in his locker
he was hiding a gun.

# RUMORS

They spread like wildfire.
They lurked in lockers,
in the gymnasium,
in the cafeteria, the library,
the study cubicles,
the dim corridors
by the wood-shop room.

Kelly's pregnant.
Clark sold beer bongs
every Saturday at
the Dunkin' Donuts
just south of the school.

They ached for release.
They yearned to be shared.

Mrs. Trenton's son
is in jail for mail fraud.
Zachary stares too long
in the locker room.

Richard has an STD.
    That new girl, Yvette,
    failed second grade.
    Twice.
        Blake has a gun.

I liked the idea
of wiggling my way
into the lives of others.
I liked to slip unnoticed
into their world, like
a burglar over a window ledge
in the dead of night,
falling softly onto carpet.

When people don't pay
attention to you,
it's easy to hear more
than anyone thinks.

I liked the idea of a gun,
its massive sense
of potential.

Blake has a gun?

I listened.
I watched.
I wondered.

# REAL

The only one
who ever said
he actually saw
Blake's gun was
Nicholas,
who refused
to talk about it
anymore.
Like a closed book,
you couldn't
read anything
from him.

Nose deep
in comics—
*Graphic novels!*
he corrected
when accused
of loving the Hulk
and Superman—
he didn't care
much about
being popular,
which he could've
been if he dared
spread his story.

But he made
the mistake of talking—
                and who wouldn't,
                with a secret this huge—
to Louis, who told Megan
and her sister, Wendy,
which meant that everyone
knew by fourth period,
and people were
staring, pointing.

That's how Blake
became of interest
to us all, a freak show
to be eyed from a distance.
Like he was a bug-eyed monster
who vomited on his lunch
before slurping it all up.
People stared.

# AARON

slammed the books
out of Blake's hands
like he was dunking
a basketball.

"Butterfingers!"
he laughed,
and I seethed
as everyone cracked up.

Then he knocked past
Blake and shouldered
me into the lockers
hard enough to make
my ears ring.

If it wasn't Aaron,
it was someone else
going spaz on us "losers."
A bully. A jock.

Some ass who needed
to be knocked down
a few dozen times.
Someone who deserved
to have teeth kicked in.

Blake sighed, then picked up
his books, straightened the spine
of *Algebra I: The Basics*,
and just walked away.

When I realized my nose
was bleeding, I just hid
in the guys' bathroom
and stuffed towel wads
up my nostril. Again.

# TRUTH

If it wasn't me
being knocked down,
it was Nicholas or Blake
or some other puny
freshman with more
acne than friends.

I should've done something
at some point to make it stop.
But I'm too much like
Shakespeare's stupid hero Hamlet:
a do-nothing whiner.

Except he's got a girl
who loves him.
   I didn't even have that.

It's an awful thing to confess—
being a coward.

# BECKY ANN

Long-limbed
and blond
like an endless
shower of starlight,
she was the love
of my life.

Worse,
everyone
knew it.
Especially her.

I made the mistake
of admitting
I found her stunning
to Joshua
in PE
three weeks
into the year.
I knew Joshua
from our old school
and thought
I could trust him.

He told
everyone,
*CJ's in looooove.*

You'd think
a kid with
cold sores
and too many
freckles
wouldn't rat
anyone out.

Joshua had friends
now, so it's hard
to blame him.

Still,
Becky Ann
didn't talk to me.
Her beautiful
silvery lips
never said
my name.
Until that Thursday.

*Andy,*
*I want to see*
*that gun,*
she whispered
into my ear,
        daring me

to steal
my father's
master keys.

As if she knew
I'd already been
thinking about it.

# THE OTHER KIDS

Most of them thought
the gun was just a big
stinking lie.
No one brought guns
to school.
Maybe in Detroit
or that part of Miami
that's pure poverty,
an area that's smoked
enough crack to kill
itself twice over.

Our school was small.
Our school was safe.
Sure, our metal detectors
were terrific at belt buckles,
cell phones, and tongue
piercings, but if the hall monitors
were out for a smoke
or traffic jammed after
a quick Wendy's run,
we didn't funnel through—
we sidled right past the sensors.
Because our school was small.
Because our school was safe.

No one brought guns here,
most of us decided.
Though a few steered
clear of Blake.
       Just in case.

They tugged their baseball caps
low over their eyes
as his shadow lurked
past, a stormy presence
that made us cower
like Coach Tom's whistle,
or the tornado siren drills,
or Aaron looming down
the hall with that gonna-get-ya
look in his eyes.

# WHAT I SAW

Riding past on my bike
toward the arcade one Saturday,
I saw someone moving atop
the second story of Jefferson High.
A copper pipe gleaming in his hand,
he brought it crashing
against an exhaust vent,
the noise scattering birds
all the way to the football field.
Then again. Again.
And again.

I paused, watching this
dark figure—Blake, I realized—
who paused too,
his shoes on the edge
as he eyed the blacktop below.
I shielded my eyes against
the afternoon glare
and wondered if this was
the moment before a wild leap,
testing fate, or faith.

Blinking, I realized Blake was gone,
and I told myself I'd imagined it.
Who'd do such a thing? I wondered,

but then I thought of ham-fisted Aaron,
the cheerleaders who laughed at "all those dumb geeks,"
and the sophomore backup QB
who called Blake "a big-time queer."

# WORLD OF WARCRAFT

I played it more
than I should've,
sometimes
all weekend,
especially
when Dad
took Mom
to see Grandma,
who usually
didn't remember
to put in her
good teeth
and hasn't
remembered me
since last July.

I just pleaded
asthma issues
so I could stay home,
then plugged in
for hours.

I killed wave
upon wave
of undead
warriors,

blasting them
to smithereens,
wondering
if Blake ever
played World
of Warcraft,
and if he did,
was he the type
to tiger-stalk
my gnome rogue
and slay him,
taking a pipe
to my head
like a two-handed
sword shrouded
in golden flames?

My shrink, Dr. Zigler,
once said games
were a "reasonable outlet
for pent-up aggression."

I clicked the perfect
combination
and the screen
became an inferno,

its orange glare
too bright
to look straight at.

Ka-BOOM.

# GRANDMA

Mom tried to see her
a few times each month.

She wished it could be
more, but it's so terrible
to see someone wasting
away like they're being
devoured from the inside out.

They cried a lot, both Mom
and Grandma, each unable
to voice the agony
that had become their lives.

They didn't make me visit
any longer, as if that made
any of it less real.

# WHEEZE

Between gym and English,
I felt the breath whoosh out
of my lungs. I usually forgot
my inhaler, but not that day.

I sucked down the medicine
and stood there, leaning against
the wall of lockers, watching
everyone stream past—
a river of kids heading every
direction but toward me.

If I went blue in the face
and lay gasping on the floor,
would anyone even dial 911?

# PROMISE

Becky Ann
ignored me
for days and
days and forever,
so I thought she
must not have
meant it, or perhaps
I merely imagined
her breathy request
to see if Blake
really had a gun.
But then, like a boundless
dream bursting
to life, she cornered
me at the 7-Eleven
after school,
and I stood there,
a doofus holding
a sizzling bean-
and-cheese burrito,
my Big Gulp
spilling over
unnoticed
while her three
friends looked
through the magazine rack.

Becky Ann leaned in close
and purred, *Do this for me,*
*I'll do something*
*for you.*

My throat shut
as I watched them
saunter into her
older sister's
blue convertible.
They roared away,
laughing freely,
as loneliness stabbed
through me again,
a steel needle
pushed slowly
into my skull.

*I'll do it!* I yelled
as I ran outside.
They were half
a block away
and moving fast.
*I swear I will!*

# BELIEF

Most days,
I just wanted
to avoid
looking bad.

Sometimes,
though,
I wanted to
look good.

With Becky Ann
at my side,
it'd all have been
so different.

Like hitting
an earth-sized
RESET button
or getting
a bonus life.

What better way
to rack up a high
score than that?

# THE KEYS

Dad kept them
on a huge steel
ring at his hip.

The master keys.
They opened everything
at our school.

You could hear
him approaching
by their jingle.

> *Cling, clang,*
> *Mr. Clean.*
> *Cleans up soup,*
> *Smells like poop.*

> *Cling, clang.*
> *Jing, jang.*
> *Loop-de-loop,*
> *Smells like poop.*

And so on.

How many
other kids' dads
had songs about them?

# PETE

My father's part-time help,
Pete, worked three hours each
morning and skipped out early
once in a while through
the band-room door.
My father wished he had
full-time help, which he needed,
even though our school
was a hundred and fifty less
than capacity. *REAL full-time help*,
my father muttered over a mop
after hours one day,
cursing the kids who
exploded ketchup packets
all over the cafeteria floors.

*I'll help*, I said to him,
watching the keys on his hip
jingle on the thick D-ring.
He told me to concentrate on
homework so I'd never have
to worry about cleaning floors
or repairing rooftop exhaust vents.
I didn't stare at $x^2 + 3 = 28$
but watched those keys
wink at me, clink at me,
beckon as if they were made of pure silver.

# BLAKE

A few of the science teachers
were crabbing about him
in the teacher's lounge
while I waited for my father
to take me home. I sipped my Coke
in the corner, ignored again.
"Wack job," one said.

This was how people talked
about him behind his back.
I started to really worry about
what people said when I
wasn't around.

I don't know
if I really wanted
to see if Blake
had a gun
or whether
I just wanted
to impress Becky Ann
by having the guts
to go look.
    Who knows what
    the "something"
    she promised
    would be?

Remembering how
every day after lunch
she eased a single
square of strawberry
Bubble Yum
from the pack
and slid it
into her mouth
so slowly
made me think
of a praying mantis,
and how the females

leisurely devour
their mates alive.

Maybe I imagined
myself a hero,
saving the school
from a wack job,
though Blake
didn't look
like a wack job—
just a hollow-eyed
kid whose father
never came back
from Iraq.

But I started
to wonder.
I'd only seen
a gun on TV,
never in person.

Maybe Nicholas
was lying.
Maybe there
was no gun.

Surely the teachers
would know
if a kid had a gun.

Surely someone
would do something.

Then I realized:
what if
        *I*
were that
        someone?

# MATH CLASS

Instead of moaning
over memorizing
the rules of geometry,
I considered Blake
across the room,
how he slumped
in his second-row desk
and yawned, scratching
a giant ☺ into its face
with a set of keys.
Was that really him
I'd seen atop the school,
going berserk?
And even if so,
                so what?

Kids busted up windows, spray-
painted fences, and broke streetlights
with rocks all the time.
I'd smashed up my share
of things and had even once let
the air out of Dr. Trimbourne's tires
after two days of detention
for spitballs I didn't shoot.

Blake wasn't any different
from anyone else with

a dead dad, I decided.
I thought about Grandma
withering away upstate
in a hospice.
It's not the same,
dying slow versus BOOM
being killed. But dead is dead,
and I tried to imagine
someone close to me
being gone forever.
Mrs. Cullerton, our neighbor
who bakes us rhubarb pies.
Grandma. My dad.

Would I act any differently
from Blake if I woke up
one morning and they weren't
there? Would people make up
stories about me to make
themselves feel better?

# LUNCH

Becky Ann's brushing her hair,
but I'm unshirting her
again in my mind,
me and a half dozen other
kids with candy-glazed
eyes who no longer saw
cell phones and ice cream
sandwiches but simply
a bright orange brush
pulled through the rivulets
        of her amazing hair.

When the guidance
counselor, Mr. Green,
said, *Andy? Everything
going all right?*
I dog-paddled out of
the ocean of my desire,
saying, *I'm fine I'm fine,
why wouldn't I be fine?*

I read that every boy
between twelve and twenty
thinks of sex
        every
              seven
                    seconds.

Maybe Mr. Green
sensed this since
he is a guy, after all,
but I probably helped
skew that statistic,
thanks to Becky Ann.

# MR. GREEN

We called him Mr. Green,
but he's barely older
than my cousin Luke,
who's on scholarship
for lacrosse at U of M.

Mr. Green meant well.
He tossed a Frisbee
and joked with us after school.
He wandered the halls
between periods.

He tried to get along,
talked Jaguars trivia with
the jocks, but he's not
one of us, so no one tells him
anything. Not really.

Sure, he sat down with Blake,
whose father died this past June,
the explosion supposedly strong enough
to blow out windows a block away.
Sure, Mr. Green cared.

But Blake swore he was fine,
the same lie any of us would've told
to a counselor or a teacher

who didn't know not to believe it.
No one breathed a word
to Mr. Green about a gun.

Mr. Green saw the world in bright
colors—he imagined people as good.
He didn't notice the bullying,
the desk graffiti, the kids who
stank of smoke and beer.

Mr. Green truly meant well,
and that, at least, was something.

# GOING AFTER THE GUN

You get an idea

like that in your head,

it's pretty much impossible

to shake free of it.

# HEALTH CLASS

Well-armed with sexual
jargon after the two-week
barrage from Mrs. Drummond,
the science teacher,
we still tittered over
*scrotum* and *nipples*,
watched encore videos
on self-examination
and the 72-hour life
of Mr. Sperm. Even
the teen pregnancy
scare tactics fueled
our desire instead
of dousing its flames.

No surprise that I,
ignoring well-deserved shame
over my 24/7 desire
for Becky Ann,
thought not of babies
and diapers, gonorrhea
or safe sex,
but of silk panties,
denim skirts, and silver-
painted toenails.

I knew then
I'd do anything
for the "something"
she promised.
I knew that gun
was going to be
the turning point
of my world.

My salvation.

And if Blake REALLY
had it, I knew
just how to find it.

# SICK

Surrounded
by pale blue tile,
Dad lingered
in the tub,
his uniform
forgotten
on the floor.
And right there, too,
the ring of keys.

      He couldn't stop
      coughing.
      I couldn't stop
      myself.

My heart
zigzagging,
I brought him
chicken soup
and a thermometer.
Tylenol as well.

      When he shut
      his eyes and
      sank into the steaming
      water right up
      to his face,

I pocketed
　　the keys.

Mom was napping,
tired after another
argument over
moving her mother
to a better place,
one we couldn't afford
since she couldn't find
better part-time work
than the drugstore,
and our insurance
company again said,
*No.*　　*No.*　　*No.*

Lousy paychecks
and lousier insurance
were the same reason
I hadn't met with
Dr. Zigler, my therapist,
in forever. I saw her
two weeks back through
the smudged glass
of Denny's front window.
She returned to her scrambled
eggs without waving.

The keys clinked
so loud I thought
I heard a hundred
kids screaming,
    *Cling, clang,*
    *Mr. Clean!*

                I waited,
             listened for
         his breath,
      which didn't
             falter,
        and wondered
       if it were
     this easy.

He didn't hear.
Aching,
throbbing,
congested,
he didn't
notice anything
but his own
sinus agony.

Stealing from
your father—

there should be
unbearable weight,
bloodied knuckles,
distress way back
in your eyeballs.

Instead I felt nothing
but the dizzying roar
        of excitement.

# THAT NIGHT

The window opened
without screeching,
and no police sirens
wailed to life nearby.
I sucked on my inhaler, then
slid soundlessly over the sill
and dropped to the grass,
so cool on my bare knees.

In dark shorts and T-shirt,
I stole through the neighborhood
and jogged the mile and a half
to school, dodging the bright
headlights, streetlights, anything
that might give me away.

I'd never considered security
systems, the howl of blame
that might erupt when I
opened the steel door
by the school's loading dock.
There wasn't a sensor.
Not there, at least.

I eased inside and became
one of the shadows, moving

slowly through the muted darkness
of the hallways until I found
his locker. The keys heavy
in my hand, Becky Ann
had to know. I had to.

# LOCKER

In my own
locker, I kept
a red plastic
jug of loose change
and Becky Ann's
old white hairbrush
that she left in the girls'
locker room—
I found it when
helping Dad wax
the floors one Sunday
and recognized
the faint memory
of her fragrance.

Four different textbooks,
two spiral notebooks,
five #2 pencils,
a mirror, a poster
of Peyton Manning
in a U of Tennessee
uniform, and two
empty boxes
of Thin Mints.

Plus three clean socks,
though I once had

three full pairs.
Scissors. Gum eraser.
Bic pens—two blue,
one black, and one
that might've been red
though it just leaked
dark ooze on everything
now. I kept that one
wrapped in a paper towel
in the back.

I have
a hard time
throwing anything
away.

# UNLOCKED

Blake's locker?
I touched its cold steel face,
the mealy gray that my father
repainted each summer.
I spun the black dial,
tried my birthday,
the grade I got on
my last math test,
my own locker combination.

Nothing worked,
which was no surprise.
I don't know why I
wanted to try the dial.
Maybe it just felt
less dishonest.

Then I used the keys.

No alarms exploded
through the halls.
It was just me in after-
school darkness,
the welcome quiet
of unopened books,
empty halls, and
teacherless rooms.

Open at last, Blake's
locker didn't emit
some funky smell
like Sue's had
when she forgot a banana
inside during fall break.

Blake had the same books
I did, the same little metal shelf
on top. A Florida Marlins hat.
Some blank notebook paper.
A paper-clip chain dangling
from the coat hook.

I rooted through it all,
cataloging it,
running my fingertips
across everything
like I was reading Braille.

No gun.

I swallowed thickly.
What were we thinking?

# BECAUSE

I did not do drugs . . .
I did not date . . .
I did not drive . . .
I was not crowded with friends . . .
my parents did not let me have a job . . .
even Dr. Zigler didn't get me . . .
my father was our school's janitor . . .
I'd been bullied for six years straight . . .

      I stole those keys.

I wanted something that mattered
to the cool kids at school.
Rebel courage.
Bad-boy stuff.

But even that got screwed up.

# CAUGHT

My dad
found out
about the keys,
just like he knew
somehow
when I'd snagged
three Michelobs
last December
from his minifridge
in the garage.

I tried to sneak
the keys back
the next morning,
but he caught me.
I said I was just
looking at them,
just checking them out,
    but he knew
I'd taken them.

No iPod.
No TV.
No Warcraft.
No teachers' lounge Cokes.
No trust.

After school,
I had to wait
on a hard
plastic chair
near the principal's
office now,
so Ms. McGee,
the secretary,
could watch me.

One day,
she slipped
me a Hershey's Kiss.
It helped.
    But not much.

# WHY

Dad didn't ask at first,
but finally did, hollering,
*What the HELL were you thinking?*

No answer would satisfy
that type of question, so
I simply shrugged, pressing

the truth quietly to my heart.
Wrong move. He looked at me,
his anger a cold, steady rain.

*Grounded for life*, he finally snarled,
and I knew Mom would eventually
calm him down, but not anytime soon.

I should've told him something else.
Maybe honesty would've worked.
I was curious. Concerned. Worried?

But that wasn't true. I was excited
and hopeful. I wanted to find that gun.
I wanted in on a big-time secret.

I wanted to shake up my life
like a cup of Dungeons & Dragons dice
and reroll, but even that was denied me.

got caught cheating
on a sociology test,
and that got me thinking—
maybe he lied about
the gun all along?

Rumors burst to life
like summer fires
in a forest of kindling.
Whisper that secret
to two or three people
like Nicholas did,
and everyone—
        I mean everyone—
knew.

But the week's worth
of detention made him
a little more popular.
Sue, in particular,
suddenly noticed him.

I stole the keys and my
straight-shooter dad
confessed to the school.
He got docked two days' pay,

I got grounded, and
none of the other kids
believed how brave I was,
no matter how much I
tried to convince them.

# DR. ZIGLER

Not only was I positive that
we couldn't afford more sessions,
but I knew I couldn't tell her
          the truth.

So we stared at each other
across the long brown couch,
the clock ticking at a dollar a minute
as I told her about reading Tolkien,
playing Halo, and how Sue
got a purple neck tattoo
of a three-headed dragon.

Thinking of Sue made me
think about her new boyfriend, Nicholas,
who wasn't such a total loser anymore,
which made me want to kick him—
anyone, really—right in the nuts.

# ANGER

No one believed me.
Becky Ann refused
to catch my eye
during passing periods,
her fruit-scented breath
hot on my face
like an accusation
that I was lying about it all.

*Lie about what?*
*Going into his locker?*
*Not finding the gun?* I asked.
But she twirled her hair
magnificently
as I watched her tramp away.

Bruce said I was too scared
of my father to have taken
the keys. My father was
indeed a big, big man.

Romeo just laughed
at me. *Jesus H. Christ,*
*CJ—you're an idiot.*

I was furious
with myself

for doing it.
And not just because
Becky Ann's loyalty
was stunningly
inconsistent.

I was angry
for being
an idiot.
A fool.

I was angry
that nothing
I did ever
worked out
right.

# DR. ZIGLER

Two grueling Saturday sessions
and Dad let me stop going.

Maybe it's the janitor in him, but
he takes waste personally.

# CONFRONTATION

*Did you actually see it?*
I repeated to Nicholas
that Friday after school
while he unlocked his bike.

He noticed too many
people noticing us together,
my voice a little too loud.

*Dude, just leave me alone.*
            *C'mon!*
Then he pedaled away.

Nothing like a former loser
snubbing you to make you feel
about three inches tall.

# TRUST

It's like
everything
in your life
is a fat powder keg,
and somehow
you discover a fuse
and accidentally
       light it.

Blow as hard
as you want,
douse it with spit,
    pinch it,
snip the fuse clean off,
scream for help—
still it burns
and burns and burns
and BOOM.
         Gone.

And you might as well
be gone too, for all
the good you are
to anyone,
pathetic thing
that you've become.

# LUNCH

Becky Ann's crowd
razzed me so often that
I started eating
outside my father's
office, the janitor room
back by the gym.
It stank of disinfectant
and chemicals and sawdust
and God-knew-what,
which made every lunch
miserable, but at least
no one would look for me there.

Everyone knew how embarrassed
I was by my father's job—
almost as much as I was
by the whole gun fiasco.
After a few days, it seemed
no one really missed me at all,
which didn't prove all that shocking.
The days of shame accumulated
like dead insects in a light fixture.
Wishing things were different,
I ate cold salami sandwiches alone,
imagining my life as a path
that miraculously turned back
on itself, giving me another chance.

# EARLY OCTOBER

The rains stayed
for three days,
which had my dad
mopping nonstop
at the slop and mud
kids dragged in on
their boots and clothes.
I felt like running away
and living on a farm
in Iowa where I could
sweat away the days
under a bright, unflinching
sun and surround myself
with a world of green,
growing things. Here
in north Florida, nothing
wholesome seemed to grow—
there's just the slow stink
of too many bodies
resenting each other.
I've had enough of that.

# CONFESSION

*It's okay,*
Blake told me
right before fifth period
one Wednesday.
This was three weeks
after the whole
school knew
I broke into
his locker.

We're friends now.
At least a little.
One day he just
walked up to me
and sat down
to eat gumdrops
out of his shirt pocket.
We didn't talk
beyond those two words.
We rarely talked.

I never asked him
if he had a gun.
What made me believe
an idiot like Nicholas?

Done with trying
to calm my father's
displeasure,
I now sat with Blake
during lunch.
We were satisfied with
silence while
the other kids
drank chocolate shakes
and ate french fries,
laughing at what sounded
like hilarious jokes.

*It's okay*,
Blake repeated
above the hubbub
and noise of the world,
as if trying
to convince us both.

# BLAKE'S FAMILY

At the grocery store
where I'd gone to buy
Diet Sprite for my mom
and root beer for me, I saw him
with his mother and a little girl,
who couldn't be older than six.
His mother had shoes like
the type my mom always wore.
And she walked far too fast,
half-dragging the sister.
Blake followed too,
a small boat puttering along
the sea of linoleum,
his throttle jammed, stuck on low.

I hid behind the chip rack
and tried to imagine
my dad being dead
like Blake's dad, his body
stuffed inside a coffin.
His sister stumbled just then.
She banged face-first
into a stack of creamed
corn like a bad cartoon collision.
I almost laughed, but
the impulse murdered
itself in my throat.

I left without saying anything,
without the soda, without
any sense of what was
funny anymore.

# BLAKE'S MOM

I tried to think
what it was like
for her. The only
way I could come

close was to picture
my mom, then
subtract half
of her happiness.

When Grandma
eventually surrendered
to her sickness,
would Mom charge
through grocery stores too,
not noticing if I was behind her
or not?

# TUTOR

Though my math teacher, Mr. Oliver,
said I needed three hours
of help a week, my father
got the idea that another student
from my class would be cheap,
"and you'd both already have the same books!"

So Sue became my tutor.
Mostly she just picked zits
off the back of her neck
as she explained polynomials
like she had learned them
from the same boring book
Mr. Oliver did, and I couldn't
understand them any better from her.
Sometimes she muttered about Nicholas
and their on-and-off-again status.
The idea of them both finding love
rubbed me about as wrong as
the stupid math problems did.

*For eighteen bucks an hour,*
*you WILL pay attention*, my father
insisted after he saw me doodling
instead of slaving away in my notebook.
So I pretended, but I was getting more
weary by the day of people

telling me what I should
and should not do. Of people
finding friends, finding love,
but not me. I was fourteen,
not four. And I wasn't
half as useless as people seemed
to take me for. Including Sue,
who rolled her eyes regularly
when she wasn't checking out
that new tattoo in her pocket mirror.

# REVELATION

Sue slammed shut the books one afternoon
and just cut me this look that said,
*Why are we wasting our time?*

Damned if I knew.

# VISIT

One Saturday, Blake
just showed up
at my place.
We sat in the living
room on the stupid
hand-me-down couches
and drank iced tea.
*They stole my gym*
*uniform again*, he
said as I flipped channels
on the TV. The gun rumors
kept buzzing despite
what I learned, but people
still pushed Blake around,
still poured cafeteria milk
into the slats of his locker,
and still sometimes threw his
gym stuff in the trash.
I'm not sure who
had it worse.

Mom knew it was rare for anyone
to swing by, so she let us play
Halo for an hour. Blake wasn't
very good, but we had fun anyway.
Mom invited him to stay for lunch—
sloppy joes, big deal—

but Blake said he just wanted
to meet my family and had to get home
before his mother got back
from the YMCA.

*He seems well-mannered,*
my mom said when he left.
Dad didn't say anything—
he was still fuming over me stealing
his keys, a stupid game
of daring and theft
he thought I had played alone.
What would he think
if he knew Blake's part in it?
Or Becky Ann's?

# MISTAKES

Who hasn't made
a million of them?

My fourth-grade art disaster,
the Popsicle castle
with too many turrets.

Bleaching my hair
in fifth grade.

Riding my bike
off that ramp last summer
with my eyes screwed
shut on a dare.

Telling Aaron Andrews
that he had stink breath.

Stealing the keys?
So far, my worst.
                So far.

# BLAKE

Maybe once my video-game ban
was lifted for good, I'd get Blake
to play Warcraft with me.
You need gaming partners
to get through the toughest dungeons,
and who else did I have to play with?

My self-doubt kicked to life, and I wondered
if Blake truly enjoyed my company as much as
I enjoyed his. It's frustrating as all hell,
but I'm often incapable of understanding
what people around me are actually feeling.

The filters and veils and delusions
are just too tough for me to pierce.
That's pretty much all I took away
from Dr. Zigler's sessions—I was a screw-up
who didn't cope well with the real world.

Big news flash.

# MCDONALD'S

We went to the one on Fifth
at least once a week after school.
Blake rarely brought his books,
but I sometimes studied
while we shared fries and
came up with suggestions
on what Sue's new tattoo should be,
as well as where it should go.

My favorite: holster and six-shooters
around the waist in purple ink.

His favorite: a black barbed-wire noose
around the neck.

# SNAKE

Everyone knew
I was ophidiophobic
after Romeo brought
Hermes, his brother's
ball python, to school
last year for a Halloween prop
and I eeked girlishly,
earning me the nickname
"Andy-pansy." Which stuck.
Thank you so very much, Sue,
who still called me that
during tutoring sessions
when Dad and Mom weren't around.

So when I saw the slick
black skin of the striped snake
coiled inside the base of my locker—
forced through the air vents,
or perhaps someone else
made off with the master keys too,
or worked a crowbar or something—
I stumbled back, throat closing,
my face reddening as I
feared fangs, strangulation,
venom, unblinking eyes.

It was dead. Romeo
stopped guffawing long enough
to poke it with his finger
to assure me. Then the passing period
was over and I was alone
with the dark, ropy corpse.
I thought of how my father
might calmly remove the body,
then use industrial-strength
germicides to scour out
the smell, and I knew
I couldn't let him do that.

I propped the emergency door
open—the alarm's been on the fritz
for weeks, my dad complained—
and managed that snake all the way
to the tree line. Then I emptied my locker,
tore free all the snake-scented
book covers and dumped
most everything into the trash,
all my carefully hoarded stuff
added to the crumpled (unsent)
love notes, inkless pens,
and sticks of unchewed gum.

Then on hands and knees,
using brown bathroom paper
and sudsy alien-green soap,
I labored at the cold metal,
praying to get the memory
of that poor trapped snake
out before its claustrophobia
became my own.

# ANOTHER LIE

I had to throw my backpack away—
the stink of garter snake
               was never scrubbing free.
               Ma asked me where
the backpack went,
and I had to lie. Again.
               And again and again.
               Like Dr. Zigler warned,
I continued to nail myself
inside the cramped coffin
               I'd built for myself,
               the lies upon lies
becoming beetles scuttling
free over my face in the dark.
               Hungrily.

# BLAKE

Blake and I agreed to meet
at the Sbarro at the mall
instead of McDonald's for once.
It was supposed to be
another math-tutoring deal,
but Sue really just wanted
to sneak off with Nicholas,
so she paid me to shut up about it.
So I bought the pizza and the Cokes
while Blake and I listed the top
ways to get back at Aaron for jamming
that dead snake inside my locker.
My favorite? Duct-taping him naked
to the flagpole an hour before school started.
Blake preferred a good case of crotch rot
and perhaps a black magic curse.
He waved his arms and in a thick voice said,
*May the fleas of a thousand camels*
*infest your armpits!*
I had to be home by 6:30,
only we were cracking up so much
that I didn't make it home until 8.

# HALLOWEEN

Though far too old to trick or treat,
I still hustled door to door
with Blake, both of us
dressed in bedsheets
with snipped-out eyeholes,
ghosts à la Charlie Brown.
We moaned and *oooOOOO*ed
and Blake clanked a bike chain
he brought along,
which scared all heck
out of some third graders—
two Spidermans, a hobo,
and some kind of orange lizard.
Our paper grocery sacks
filled fast with candy,
though most knew we
were too tall, too old
to really be out. But no one
minded since we were just
loading up on sugar and not
hitting car windows with eggs.
For three hours, we were regular kids
doing regular stuff,
having a good time.
For three hours, I didn't think
about stolen keys, guilt, Becky Ann,

or what might be wrong with my friend.
For three hours, it was the happiest
I'd been in forever, unfazed
even when Blake said,

> *You ever dream that you wake up*
> *and the whole world's gone?*

# CONFESSION #2

With Thanksgiving
turkeys and Xmas trips
on everyone's mind,
no one talked about
Blake's gun
anymore.

Now he was just
CJ's weird pal,
which didn't
seem to bother
him, even when
people *SSSSSsssed*
at me in the halls,
       Aaron most of all.

Blake followed me
to school now—
I walked instead
of taking the bus.
Part of my punishment
for the keys thing.
Plus Dad always sought
ways to slim me down
since he'd always been
a little beefy himself,
my asthma be damned.

Blake even went
into the arcade
with me one Saturday.
I was supposed to be
picking up Colgate
and Kleenex at Target.
More errands, more
punishment.

My cell phone kept buzzing,
but I didn't answer Mom's
calls. Trouble was trouble—
how much worse could it get?

Blake didn't play Pop-A-Shot
or Mortal Kombat
or even the NASCAR game,
where I mostly just rammed head-on
into every road sign I could.
He just watched
me push quarters
into the machines
for two hours.

On the way home,
my pockets empty,
he pushed it into my hands.

*It's a Beretta 9mm.*
*My father kept it*
*in the closet in a box*
*with the Christmas lights.*

I gave it back,
almost astonished
my hands didn't
explode into flame.

I never made it to Target.
Instead, I took three puffs
on my inhaler and told Blake
I was late getting home.
And I ran.

# ASKING

Some kids, my father
just didn't trust.
He swore he had
a special radar about
troublemakers,
and he was usually right.

He knew Jorge
was "bad news,"
and that was before
the smoke bomb
put the girls' bathroom
out of commission for three days.

He wasn't surprised
when the Murray twins
got expelled for punching out
a seventh grader from the Montessori school
across the street, or when Nicholas
swiped three rolls of quarters
from the cafeteria cash register
and got caught the same day
with two ounces of pot.

My father put down
the mop one afternoon
and knelt to look me

right in the eyes,
the type of piercing gaze
that might allow him
to scrutinize my actual thoughts.

The air reeked
of piney disinfectant,
which then made me
think of snakes
writhing inside
the murk of my locker,
the dark beneath my bed,
the tunnels of my stomach.

He asked me
what was wrong
with Blake.
He knew now
about Blake's father
from Mr. Green,
who was concerned
about Blake, but not
as much as he was about
the Murray twins, Aaron,
and others who had volcanic
outbursts instead of Blake's
slow, slow burn.

My father was asking me
something else entirely.
    He knew it.
    I knew it.

I thought
of the gun,
the 9mm Beretta,
oil black and thick
in the handle.

I thought of how afraid
Blake looked
when I passed the gun
back to him, like he was
about to be devoured
by a rabies-mad grizzly.

I thought of what it meant
that he trusted me enough
to show me the Beretta,
that we hung out at McDonald's,
that he texted me daily—
usually it was nothing important,
but sometimes
what he wrote
felt storm-cloud dark.

I thought of how many months
I'd wasted slugging away
at computer games and trying
to crack the code my father used
to filter out Internet porn.

I thought of how Sue
had a new song for me now,
one that rhymed *fool* with *tool*.

I thought of how Aaron had run
Blake's latest new pair
of gym clothes up the school flagpole.

I thought of the tough-guy attitude
I wished I'd had but knew—
just *knew*—that I didn't.

I thought of how long
I'd longed to see that gun,
and how it was the key
to a door still shut before me.

I said, *Nothing*.

# THE OTHER JANITOR, PETE

was
fired, let
go one day.
"Disciplinary
reasons." Just
given two weeks'
notice, which drove
my dad batty, since this
year's budget, already so
far in the red, wouldn't allow
a replacement until next year. The
workload, though, wouldn't let up, which
meant he had even more to do himself. He
didn't complain. He didn't punch locker doors.
He just did what he had to do. Silently. Reluctantly.
And so I remained Blake's only friend. Silently. Happily.
Wishing my father—for one damn second—would be proud of me.

# FIRING IT

The old lot
where the Winn-Dixie
once stood
was perfect.

It wasn't yet dusk,
but the clouds
made it seem so.

Not two miles from
Fairmont Heights,
where I lived,
we lined Coke cans
on the old metal
guardrail, gouged
and bent from
so many run-ins
with mishandled carts.

Ammo clinked
in his pocket
like nails spilling
down stairs.

He said it'd be fun.
He aimed and those cans
danced. Some exploded.

Sometimes he missed,
and the ground way
back against the hill
ruptured as if a ghost
were slamming a fist
into the hard earth.

A crow lazed
overhead toward
a dead streetlight.
Blake aimed
and yelled, *POW!*
*POW! KA-BLAM!*

He didn't shoot,
though. He didn't
actually fire
at the bird, which
eventually vanished
into the cluster
of shadows by the dump.

When he offered me a try
with the gun, I held it,
thinking about everything
and nothing all at once.

Without firing,
I gave it back,
my breath held tight
in my chest.

He reloaded.
I sat and watched,
afraid to get up,
as if I might
slide and crack
my skull open
on some imperceptible ice,
even though it was
only mid-November
here in Florida.

# THE GUN

Was it wrong
to squeeze my eyes shut
and think about it
all night, its dark shine,
its potent, peculiar bulk?

What would Dr. Zigler say?
I wondered that night,
then decided I didn't
give a damn.

# NOTHING

Becky Ann didn't believe me,
even when I vowed
I could bring it
to her after school.
Blake offered to loan
it to me. She *Yeah, right*ed
and sped off, her heels
clicking all the way
down the hall.

The "something" she'd promised
apparently meant "nothing,"
which, to someone
who desired her so fiercely,
was worse than nothing,
which was what I was
content with prior
to her revving up my heart
with her short skirts
and oh-so-sexy smile.

But at least I had Blake,
meaning a friend,
meaning something
loads better than nothing.

And I had the gun too.

Who knows why
contemplating it
impressed me so.

Maybe "excited"
is closer to what I felt.

# FATHER ISSUES

I knew what Dr. Phil
would've said.

You loaf through enough
daytime TV with your mom

      when you're skipping school
      a few days for a fake migraine,

and you watch *Oprah*
just because it's on.

      Maybe Blake and I bonded
      because of our shared "daddy issues."

Blake's daddy? Dead.
My daddy? "Emotionally absent."

      But here's where Dr. Phil's
      homespun smarts had it wrong.

Even Dr. Zigler's psychobabble
missed the mark on this.

      What Blake and I had
      was a 9mm Beretta.

Its secret. Its high-impact ammo.
Its dark, smooth weight.

      You share a secret like that,
      you belong to something

greater than yourself,
a sky full of lightning

      that could split the world
      in half at any moment.

Most go their whole life
without knowing that kind

      of power, that kind
      of wild potential energy.

# MOM

After a few weeks of normalcy,
Mom started crying again. A lot.
Words started streaming over into tears,
just like she did when she pleaded
with God over Grandma's health.

I swore I was sorry, am sorry,
and tomorrow will still be sorry
I stole the keys and forced my own
parents to stop trusting me,
and I more or less meant it too,
but even as the words slid out, I knew
I'd meet with Blake later
to touch the gun again and
feel it buck in my hands
like it had a spirit of its own
as we emptied a box or two
into cans, bottles, telephone poles.

To think she believed me enough
to feel bad about canceling
my Warcraft account
and giving the iPod
to Cousin Ricky in Chicago,
who she felt sorry for,
her sister being so poor.

I almost told her then,
knowing that if anyone
would get it, it'd be the person
who splintered ice with a meat hammer
and fed me slivers all day
when I had that fever, or who
struggled with me all summer
to make sure I wasn't held back
thanks to my brain's insistence
that $A^2 + B^2$ did NOT equal $C^2$.

I almost told her.

# MARCH 5

Blake had the day
blacked out—
not circled
or starred,
blacked out—
on a calendar
in his locker.
No, I didn't break
in again. I just
saw it obliterated
with a Sharpie
when he went
to the bathroom
and I wanted
to see if my birthday
would fall on
a weekend
for once.
It didn't.
The bell rang,
and Blake
slammed
the locker
shut as he
shuffled off
to social studies.
I never asked him

what it meant.
Friends don't
interrogate
each other.

# HOME

I had never visited Blake's home before
and quite suddenly wanted to see it,
all the more because he told me never
 to come by there.

I wasn't all that hot on having people over either.
If my parents weren't pissed off or just being themselves—
as embarrassing as letting a fart slip in church—
our place was too small, too dingy, too pathetic.

Sure, I knew his neighborhood, though.
The lawns were golf-course green,
and an ex-cop manned the thick iron entry gate.

His father had been some type of defense contractor
prior to that car bomb that made all the headlines.
From the look of this area, he made great money.

I stood shivering outside the well-manicured community,
the December wind only part of the reason,
unsure how my feet got me there to the brick wall
with iron spikes atop it in a long, sharp row.

That was his house—there. With the big white pillars.

Was he there now in his own big bed, stewing
over what to do with that gun, remembering

the powder flash so hot on his hands, the Beretta's
thunder still echoing in his mind?
Or was that just me?

# MIDTERMS

I tanked the math test.
After class, Mr. Oliver asked
if I'd flunked on purpose.
*No*, I told him, knowing
he'd come down hard on Sue,
his best student.
*I just suck at math.*

At least I got an A in English.
My creative assignment about
the boy who could shoot laser beams
out of his eyes and saved the world
seemed to impress Mrs. Hawkins,
who had published three short stories
of her own, she repeatedly assured us.

One A, three Bs, a C, and an F.
My father fired Sue (thank God!)
and threatened me with Catholic school
like my mom had suffered through (and still hated).
She told me it wasn't a real threat
but that I needed to do better.
*Just try*, was what she pleaded.
*Just give us an honest effort.*

When she wasn't sobbing,
Mom could be pretty persuasive.

That word again buzzed
angrily in my ears. *Honest.*

# CHRISTMAS

Blake was gone
for three weeks.
Aspen, I think.
Somewhere you
could ski all day
and sleep away
the nights in log cabins
with immense fireplaces
and wide-canopied beds.

We stayed home
and suffered through
a freak ice storm,
which shut down everything
for twenty-four hours,
whitening this dreary place
like frosting on a dumb cake.

Blake didn't call or text, but
he later admitted that the first day there,
he plowed headfirst into
a Colorado snow bank so far
that he had to be yanked out
by the ski patrol.
The phone was lost in the hubbub,
    apparently.

I missed him. But I missed
the gun more, its terrific
kickback when it fired.
Its confidential existence.
Its ability to cement
my friendship with Blake.

I wondered if that said
something about me,
that it took a gun to do all that.

# NEW YEAR'S EVE

With my mom planning
her usual laundry list of resolutions,

1. be 8 lbs. slimmer
2. see Grandma more
3. save an extra $5 a week
   *etc. etc. etc.*

I picked at leftover turkey
and pried chunks of pineapple
off the honey-glazed ham
we weren't eating
until tomorrow night.
The TV was on—some
holiday show with orphans—
but I watched the window,
hoping for a whiteout
that never came.

March 5.
The date came back to me
like an old wart
you couldn't quite shake.
I pressed another piece
of turkey to my lips,
but it had gone cold.

I sealed it back
into the Tupperware.

March 5.
Like most unknowns,
it made me anxious.

# SPRING TERM

Blake and I started school
again like we'd never left.

We ate together, walked
the halls together, and we
fired the gun as often as three
times a week together.

I started to smell gunpowder
on my hands in school,
so I took some heavy-duty
soap from my dad's office
and scrubbed at my skin
until I was nearly bleeding.

Like trying to scour out
a memory, the gunpowder reek
didn't leave my hands.

It never occurred to me
to stop shooting the gun.

It never occurred to me
that I could hit
10 for 10 now
without
effort.

# MOM

locked herself
in the bathroom
one Saturday
and refused
to come out.
Then came
the sound of
shattering.
The mirror,
we thought.
Maybe
the hair dryer too.
And from
the sudden smell,
a perfume bottle.

*Give her some
room*, Dad said
as we went out
for ice cream.
The clamor crescendoed,
and he shrugged.
*Grief does funny
things to people.*

With Grandma
worsening daily,

I was suddenly glad
I hadn't burdened
my parents with anything
about Blake or the gun.
Crazy as my mom
had become,
she'd probably
throw me in jail herself.

# AT BASKIN-ROBBINS WITH MY FATHER

*When I was maybe sixteen,*
Dad began, shutting his eyes
as if that helped him remember
himself as anything but a uniformed
nitwit with his initials emblazoned
on a stupid brass belt buckle,
*I played the saxophone. I could*
*make that horn howl something great.*
*But then my brother and I got*
*into it and he bashed me in the face.*

One minute you're listening, I thought,
the next you're standing there like
you're buck naked in a classroom
and everyone's staring. I shifted
heel to toe, playing and replaying
the last few weeks in my head
as I licked my mint chocolate chip cone
and tried to get comfortable
in the cast-iron chairs on the outdoor patio.

My dad hasn't smoked for years,
yet right then he fished a cigarette
from his pocket, found matches,
and tore one free. He lit it slowly,
as if savoring the flame that threatened
his fingertips.

*I've never seen a saxophone around here,*
I finally said, thinking more of Blake
alone in the Winn-Dixie parking lot,
waiting to meet me later, than the distant gaze
in my dad's slate eyes.

Dad said, *I listened to your uncle*
*when he said Ma would whip us*
*for roughhousing, so we waited*
*too long before confessing. The dentist*
*couldn't set my jaw right, so that*
*was that.* He sucked lazily on the cigarette,
the smoke leaking marvelously from
his nostrils between his words.
*I wasted time,* he said, *and now*
*time wastes me.*

*Why are you telling me this?* I asked,
mesmerized by this image of a man
I began to realize I didn't know at all.
　　*Cling, clang,*
　　*Mr. Clean.*
　　*Cleans up soup,*
　　*Smells like poop.*

*Because you're a man,* he told me
as he stubbed out his cigarette

in what was left of his strawberry sundae.
The butt sizzled, then finally went cold.
*And it's okay for a man to know life*
*is full of choices, and most of the*
*ones we make are wrong.*

# BAD MONDAY

Aaron must've had the mother of them
because he tore through the hallways
that morning, knocking freshmen flat
without stopping to enjoy it. Blake
didn't see the tornado coming, his head
inside his locker. Aaron kicked
the locker door shut on Blake hard enough
to leave my friend clutching his throat,
gasping like he was the one with asthma, not me.

# TEXTS

Blake didn't answer my texts
about shooting after school,
and I couldn't stop thinking
of how the cricket song
always stopped even before
we fired our first shot,
and the thick silence
settled over everything,
    expectantly.

Without warning, March 5
entered my mind again,
and it didn't leave as easily
    this time.

Especially since my dad
was bitching about
having to fix a pair
of smashed-in rooftop vents.
    Again.

# VALENTINE'S DAY

came and went
with me barely
noticing. Nothing
really mattered
the same way
anymore. All I cared
about was that gun.

I didn't think about
Becky Ann, Sue,
or anybody at all.

I didn't do the math
to learn that March 5
was only nineteen days away.

Blake grew sullen
and didn't hang out
with me as much,
but we still shared the gun.
We still had the pact
of it between us.

Aaron still knocked Blake around.
Dad was still pissed at me.
I still sucked at math.
But with the Beretta

in my hands,
the future was unwritten
instead of just a repeat
of the same loathsome
story of my past.

Let me be honest—
that gun put me in charge
of my own autobiography.

# WHAT WE DID

Becky Ann started up a Fashion Club.
Sue got a week's suspension
for selling cigarettes at school.

Nicholas broke up with Sue (again)
but won an award for a sci-fi
story in Mrs. Hawkins's class.

My dad worked longer hours
now that Pete was in Seattle,
trying to be the next Kurt Cobain.

Mr. Green tried to two-hand stuff
a basketball and fell so hard
on the playground concrete
that he had to be hospitalized.

A retired math professor from Tennessee
was hired as my tutor. When my
parents left the room, she snapped,
*Stop screwing around and learn.*

Mom started up classes
at the community college.
Painting 101, I think. And
something about ceramics.

Grandma got even worse,
fired her nurse, and told everyone
to leave her the hell alone.

Blake and I fired the gun
and talked about how much
we hated everything.

# MICHAEL JORDAN

God knows why
he brought the MJ
rookie card to school,
but when Aaron
and two others stopped
Blake in the hall to push
him around and laugh—
"Buttsmacker!" and
"Psycho-geek!" they said—
no one expected him
to shred it and toss
the confetti at Aaron's
feet before storming
past them, mumbling
under his breath as he
wrung his hands.

Just then, Nicholas emerged
from the bathroom
and saw the card's destruction.
*Dude* . . . , he said,
shaking his head.

A card like that was worth
a few hundred bucks, surely.
I knew a little about baseball

and nearly nothing about hoops,
but even I realized that an MJ card
      was sacred.

I tried to stop Blake
but he was too far gone
into whatever dark mood
had taken him. He slid
right past me and disappeared
toward the cafeteria.
For a moment, I considered
following him, but the tardy bell
rang so I just rushed into
English class instead.

After school, I tried to find Blake.
No one had seen him.
And from the hallway whispers,
that card had been the real deal.

# CARD

When I found him at the Winn-Dixie
the next evening, a pile of spent shells
littering the ground, Blake told me
it was his father's, a basketball
junkie who grew up in Chicago.

That MJ card was from an eBay auction
the week before he headed off to Iraq.
*Something to look forward to seeing again*,
he'd joked to Blake, giving him a fake
noogie at Jacksonville International,
where a 747 touched down, ready
to ferry Blake's father away forever.

He had planned on giving it to me,
which floored me, even though
the only thing I had ever collected
were bottle caps, and my dad
threw all those out when I was nine.

# HATE

Kids hated.
That's what we did.
It's what we do best.
We hate our hair,
our zits, our friends,
our parents.
We hate our hand-me-down cars,
our crappy cafeteria lunches,
our classes, our weather.

We hate, we hate,
we hate, we hate,
all no differently
than how kids
have hated
for centuries.

March 5.
It came to me
at last, thinking
so much of hate.
A little math
assured me
I was right.
It had to be
the day Blake's

father was killed.
March 5.

I told myself that.

For me,
the gun was a hobby,
though on some level
I knew that was a lie.

For Blake,
it was something
         more.
These days, he carried it
more often than not.
Even to the movies and Wal-Mart.
I hadn't thought much
of it until now,
late February.

I began to worry
about how much hate
a kid like Blake
harbored, if the mercury
of his own thermometer
ran close to the shattering point.

I began to really worry,
thinking of the list of names
my own heart wanted
to even the score with.

I began to wonder what it really was
that mortared Blake and I together.

# WHY

Everyone knows why a kid
brings a gun to school.
   Columbine. Virginia Tech.
The blossom of blood
as a head explodes.
The holy vengeance
of a thousand, thousand
wrongs suddenly righted.
   Red Lake, Minnesota.
   Northern Illinois University.

Becky Ann laughed at me
when, in an unexpected burst
of bravado, I invited her
to the Spring Fling Dance.
*When I'm dead, maybe,*
she said, yukking it up
with her pals Linda and
the less-pretty Becky.
   SuccessTech Academy.
   Bard College at Simon's Rock.

Kids mocked my father,
saying he *hace las mesas*
*spic and span*. He's not
even Latino. My grandmother's
just a dark-skinned Greek.

University of Arizona College of Nursing.
Buell Elementary.

Why didn't people tease Romeo?
He was Mexican and had a faint
lisp. Or Aaron, whose brother
was doing sixty months for grand larceny?
Or anyone anyone anyone
but Blake who ached like
his heart was an old salt mine
now emptied of all worth.
        Dawson College.
        Platte Canyon High School.

I knew what Dr. Zigler would say,
but those shrink phrases
didn't mean anything anymore.
"Stuck at denial." "Deferred closure."
"Antisocial tendencies."
Language no longer affected us.
That's the power a gun brings.
        Essex Elementary.
        Notre Dame Elementary.

Eyes shut, mouth fastened tight,
I couldn't move, couldn't
do anything but shake.

141

Everyone knows why someone
brings a gun to school.
    Inskip Elementary.
    Bridgewater-Raritan High School.

# MARCH 1

Blake read Nietzsche
regularly, even
loaned me *Twilight
of the Idols,* which
I couldn't delve more
than five pages into.

Then Blake texted:
  *if it doesn't kill us,*
  *it makes us stronger*

entirely ignoring
that everyone knows
old Friedrich
went nutso and died.

# MARCH 2

*You'll like this,*
Blake promised,
then showed me
how to jimmy open
a maintenance door
to access the roof.

Together, we stood
in the spot I'd seen him
months earlier,
tempting the ledge
with its thirty-foot drop.

He urged me to the lip,
where you could see
the points of trees below
like wide green knives.

Wow, he stood so close
that his soles were half
off into open air, defying
gravity like it couldn't touch him.

*Heights aren't my thing,*
I said. *I swear to God.*

He cut me a look. *God?*

*We stoned him to death*
*a few hundred years ago.*

Then he brought out the gun
and sat—feet dangling
into space—while he
polished the barrel with his shirt.
*Why'd you bring that here?*
I asked, thinking how trust
can disappear like a star,
vanish so suddenly
            without a trace.

Blake said, *What do you mean?*
and I realized I might as well
have asked why he liked
french fries or wore Nikes.

We stayed there for a while,
so high above the rest of the world.
I couldn't shake the feeling
that Blake was convinced
he could stroll off the rooftop
and escape unscathed.

With my Warcraft account down,
I sometimes surfed chat rooms
and just wasted away the evening
while my parents watched TV
and ate Chex Mix in bed.

Without intending to, I clicked
onto a site called Teen Help
and just stayed a voyeur
for forty-five minutes,
longing for Warcraft mayhem
and player-versus-player battles,
wishing I could reenter
a world where the strong
could toss bolts of flame
and fire lightning arrows from a bow.
A world where there were rules
and limits and boundaries.

What I got instead was a mess
of crybabies one-upping each other.
Who cared about acne
or prom dresses or study hall notes?

Finally, I typed it in as fast as I dared.
*What do you do when your friend
takes a gun to school?*

The first answer: *You tell him*
*he's quite the pistol.*

And I logged out, an idiot
for believing this was anyone's
problem except my own.

My heart thudding
away all day long
as I went class
to class, learning
nothing except
a growing appreciation
for the power of fear.

> I watched Blake
> when he wasn't
> looking at me,
> trying to see if
> anything, ANYTHING
> seemed different.

What did I expect?
Devil horns? Maniacal
laughter? A black
cowboy hat and
bandito mask?

> Mr. Oliver called on me
> again, but all I could hear
> was my own breath
> thundering in my ears,
>                 a countdown.

# I TRIED

He skipped lunch,
but I caught up
with Blake before
history class.
*What's going on?*
       I insisted.

He tried to push
past me, but I
wouldn't let him.

I said, *C'mon*,
even though
the tardy bell
had rung.

He pursed his lips
and cut me a look.
*It's not up to us
anymore.*

When he turned
and ambled
the opposite way
to his classroom,
I didn't stop him.

I just stood there
and tried to figure out
     who
           and what
he meant
             exactly.

# USUALLY

Blake followed me
home from school,
then took a crosstown
bus back to his neighborhood.

Today, he met me
near the bike rack
and said he had
"something to take care of,"
the words hanging
in the air between us
like frosty December breath.

*Okay*, I told him,
imagining boxes of 9mm slugs
and hunting knives and rifle scopes
and blood and brain matter
and screaming and sobbing.

All we'd ever shot? Cans.
And sometimes 2-liter bottles.
And one time, a dead rat.
And the telephone poles.

Why did my mind insist on
such gruesomeness?

*Okay*, I told him,
trying not to let horror
erupt on my face.
When he said, *Good-bye*,
I felt it like he'd gut-slugged me,
as if he knew that I knew.

Which maybe was what he
really wanted, after all.

# FINALLY

I hadn't had
a friend before.
Not really.

I liked how
Blake gave me
the burned fries
at McDonald's.

I liked the smell
of mint from
the pack of gum
he never opened.

I liked how he
showed me
how to aim
a pistol
with one eye closed—
    you cock your arm
        just so.

I liked that he
showed me his
secret place
atop the school—

*The only place*
*I can actually think,*
he said.

I liked how
we didn't have
to talk—we just
hung out.

He trusted me
and hated phonies.
I didn't want
him to hate me
like he hated
everyone,
everything else.

Maybe Blake let it slip
about us and the gun,
I don't know.
But Becky Ann believed now,
and I didn't want her
to keep asking me
what it felt like,
holding that heavy steel
so cold in my hand.

I didn't want
anything bad
to happen to Blake—
he lost his father.

His family had money
and the insurance payout
had left them even more,
but they didn't have
anything important.

No store-bought
Valentine's cutout cards
or sudden popularity
was antidote enough
for either of our lives.

We were two losers
who ate too much McDonald's,
played too many video games,
and had families we sometimes
wished we could trade for twenty bucks.

Plus we had a secret.

But it struck me—
Blake and I were not

the same. The toxic world
he lived in felt huge
and free at first,
but it came at a cost
I wasn't willing to pay.

My voice thready,
my pulse double time,
I puffed on my inhaler
as if it'd give me strength.

I puffed again.

# MARCH 5

That Tuesday morning,
instead of going to class,
I found my dad
in the boiler room, tearing
open a box of detergent.

Sweating from the sudden heat,
my entire body quivering,
                              I told.

# I WASN'T THERE

. . . when Blake went to the john,
washing pretzel mustard off his hands
before returning to English class.

. . . when the group of policemen
in Kevlar vests and helmets surrounded
Jefferson High, their rifle safeties off.

. . . when the SWAT team began
emptying rooms, front of the school
to the back, shuttling out streams
of terrified kids as everyone asked,
*Is it World War III? What the hell's up?*

. . . when Lieutenant Duncan of Ocala, Florida
—having realized Blake was in the bathroom,
not L103—ordered the snipers to surround
the east wing and draw a bead on Blake's forehead
as he yelled, *Hands up! Let me see your damn hands!*

. . . as Blake ducked behind the water fountain
and took out the pistol—he had it in his jacket,
the fool, as he did so often then. *Gun!* someone screamed.
         *Gun! Gun! Gun!*

. . . when Sue—who no one realized
was in the girl's bathroom—came out. The door

banged shut so loudly, it sounded like a gunshot.
Everywhere, screams.

. . . when someone fired. Blake, terrified, accidentally
fired twice into the ceiling, spraying mineral fibers
like gray snow. The SWAT team, too, was firing.
Everyone was firing.

. . . when Blake threw down the gun and balled up,
screaming, *PLEASE don't kill me! Please!*

. . . because my father hustled me out into his pickup
in the teacher's parking lot and told me to wait
with the doors locked, head down, before he told
the principal to phone 911.

. . . because my father's first instinct was to get
me out of harm's way, even though I'd put myself
there again and again for months. I chose it.

. . . because I deserted Blake, my friend, when
he clearly needed me most.

# AFTERMATH

I stayed home for two days.
I didn't want to return to school,
to see how different it was.

I kept hearing the gunshots,
the wail of so many sirens,
the chatter of police radios
and EMTs and firemen yelling.
In my sleep, in my mind, it was there.

My dad insisted, *I KNEW
that kid was off. I just knew it.*
It's what everyone said now,
as if everyone always paid attention
to Blake and had stories to compare.

He had boxes of ammo hidden
in his locker, the news anchors claimed.
And there were vague reports of
hunting knives and smoke bombs.
*He was in our home*, Mom repeated
as she paced our house. *Our home!*

The school's metal detectors were replaced
with bigger, better versions.
The hall monitors were too.

We had a policeman on campus now,
just like the high schools in Tallahassee,
Atlanta, Miami, everywhere else.

Mr. Green came back with his arm in a cast
and gave mandatory classes on integrity,
community safety, and school violence.
He told me he was proud of me.
He told me I had done something good.

The hallway tile was still bile brown.
The rows of lockers: mouse-fur gray.
The gym still stank of kid sweat and crotch.
The bullet-riddled water fountain was replaced.
But the school wasn't the same.

How could it be?

# HERO

I was given a certificate
by Principal Carson.
My father framed it
and hung it in the hallway
next to his community college diploma.
My Warcraft account got renewed,
my iPod replaced,
TV privileges returned.

March wasn't yet through,
but my life was back
on the rails again,
my mother said,
hugging me hard
as she smiled again
for the first time in forever.

Becky Ann refused
to speak to me,
called me a freak
to her pals Linda
and the other Becky,
loud enough
for me to hear.
But someone told her
to shut the heck up.
Amazingly, she did.

Kids sat with me
at lunch, asked me
to recount the whole story.
Even Sue paused to listen,
her arm still bandaged
from one of Blake's ricochets.
Even Nicholas
put down his graphic novel to hear.
They pleaded for answers:

*Was the gun big?*　　　*How many guns?*
*Did you get to fire it?*　　*Was he acting, you know, crazy?*
　　*Did he threaten you? Did he? Did he?*
*When did you REALLY know?*　*Why didn't you tell anyone sooner?*
　*Did you ever see him shoot the gun?*
　　*Did he have grenades?*　　*Was Aaron on his death list?*
　　　*Is it true that he sleeps in the closet?*

# ABSENCE

Blake didn't return to school.
After a few weeks
of lawyers and judges and doctors
and reporters and experts,
he was sent to some "facility"—
that word made me shiver—
in Phoenix, Arizona.

I imagined Blake there
in that endless dry heat,
hunched somewhere alone
in a world of hospital white,
his father's green army belt
looped twice around his waist,
an unopened pack
of Wrigley's in his fist,
uneaten gumdrops bulging
in his shirt pocket.

Everyone called me a hero,
but it didn't feel that way.

I was a snitch.
    I told on my friend.
I was a thief.
    I stole my father's keys.

I was a liar.
   I lied about it all.
I was a fraud.
   I was popular
   for all the wrong reasons.

Worse, I still yearned
for the Beretta
and all it meant to me.

   Maybe I did prevent
   a massacre—
   we'll never know.
   But I sure as hell
   know one thing.
   I lost a friend.

      I don't have
      the words
      I needed
      to calm
      my soul.

      At least
      I was
      a hero.

At least
there was
that.

# AND THEN

I started dreaming.

Always of that day
when Blake was hauled
away in handcuffs.

Sometimes of the
*Thanks for nothing!*
I wished he'd shrieked.

Sometimes of cold
rings of steel
encircling my own wrists.

With people suddenly
interested in me,
I still lived inside
the pile of my bones
and flesh,
so acutely aware
of myself
and how I buried
who I was inside
someone else's story.

Most of all, though,
I dreamed of that Beretta,

as if by holding it again
I'd still have Blake around
instead of off somewhere
where broken kids disappear to.

*What the hell's wrong with me?*
I asked myself, wishing I'd never
seen a gun, but not quite wishing
I'd remained uncool and alone
versus the center of insincere attention
from the other kids, the teachers,
     everyone.

I dream of my long-lost, simple past,
the way I used to dream of Becky Ann.
Like iron filings to a magnet.

# AFTER

The gun might've been Blake's answer,
but it wasn't mine, as much as I wanted
to grasp hard onto any answer.

Here's what I know:
    I stopped a massacre.
    I stopped a school shooting.

Perhaps that's the answer
I never expected to find.
Perhaps that ought to be
enough for anyone,
even though it meant
surrendering the only
genuine friend I ever had.

Here's what I also know:
    I miss Blake.
    But I did the right thing.

# ACKNOWLEDGMENTS

A successful book is always the product of a powerful initial vision, some careful re-envisioning and adaptation, and collaborative input from trusted sources. With that in mind, thanks to my wife for sifting through countless drafts of this book and for reminding me to "get back into the mindset of a kid." A very special "Thank you!" is deserved by Caryn Wiseman and Mary Kole at the Andrea Brown Literary Agency—their help at a crucial point in this book's evolution was invaluable and spot-on.

Most of all, thanks are due to Mary Kate Castellani, who provided both the gentle support and tough-nosed editorial feedback that this book sorely needed.

To the many others who helped along the way, a sincere and well-deserved "Thank you!"